HEAVEN'S REWARD

HEAVEN'S REWARD

Fairy Tales from China
retold by
Catherine Edwards Sadler

ILLUSTRATED BY CHENG MUNG YUN

ATHENEUM   1985   *New York*

CHINESE FAIRYTALES AND FOLKTALES can be found in varying versions in ancient Chinese texts, folklore weeklies, larger volumes published in China after Liberation in 1949, and in the volumes published outside of China in the earlier part of this century. More accessible collections include:

T'ung-hua Yü-yen Hsüan (A Selection of Fairytales and Fables): Peking, 1959

Liao Chai Chih Yi (Strange Stories from a Chinese Studio) by P'u Sung-ling (1640–1715), translated by Herbert Giles: Shanghai, 1908

Chinese Fairytales, collected by Herbert Giles: Gowan & Gray, 1911

Chinese Fairytales, being collected of Ancient Legends: Mt. Vernon, 1938

Chinese Fairytales & Folktales, collected by Wolfram Eberhard: New York, 1938

THE AUTHOR would like to thank the following people for their invaluable assistance on this book: Ying Lien of the Foreign Languages Press, Peking; Professor Bernard Solomon of the Department of Classical and Oriental Languages at Queens College, New York; Mr. Eddie Wang, Ms. Jean Pan, and Ms. Grace Ooi of the East Asian Library—Chinese Division of Columbia University, New York, and the general staff of the Harvard-Yenching Institute Library, Harvard University, Boston.

PROPER NAMES in this text have been transcribed in the Wade-Giles system of Romanization or translated directly from the Chinese.

Library of Congress Cataloging in Publication Data

Sadler, Catherine Edwards.   Heaven's reward.

CONTENTS: Heaven's reward—The little goddess—
The poet and the peony—[etc.]
1. Fairy tales—China.   [1. Fairy tales.   2. Folklore
—China]   I. Cheng, Mung Yun, ill.   II. Title.
P78.S126He   1985   84-21532
ISBN 0-689-31127-3

Published simultaneously in Canada by
McClelland & Stewart, Ltd.
Composition by Dix Type Inc., Syracuse, New York
Printed and bound by Kingsport Press, Inc., Kingsport, Tennessee
Designed by Mary Ahern
First Edition

CONTENTS

FOREWORD

---

*F*AIRY TALES the world over are a magical blend of fantasy and fact, reflecting the beliefs, ways, hopes and fears of the people from which they have sprung.

Nowhere is this more true than in the fairy tales of the Middle Country, as China is called. Its long history, rigid social structure, and huge populace of diverse nationalities has given birth to intriguing and often revealing fairy tales—tales which at different times have been the literature of the scholarly, tools for the socially rebellious, a means of expression for the oppressed and in most recent times a vehicle to rally and inspire the masses.

The oldest fairy tales reflect Confucian philosophy which was the backbone of Chinese society for a great part of its long history. Confucianism placed emphasis on structure and order. Society was based on the Emperor as son of heaven and father of the people. Beneath him was a strict hierarchy of nobles and officials. To rise in that hierarchy required the passing of official examinations. Within each level of society relationships were defined—peasant must submit to landlord, wife to husband, child to father, official to Emperor. The first tale in this collection, *Heaven's Reward* dates from the Confucian period.

Taoist philosophy challenged the established Confucian structure. At the root of Taoism was the belief in the equality of all things and the conviction that physical trappings lead away from the true path and that we must aspire toward achieving spiritual peace. *The Little Goddess's* disobedience to her father and her year of meditation were a radical Taoist rejection of Confucianism.

A wealth of fairy tales reflect the Taoist view, many written by the master storyteller, Pu Sung-Ling. *The Poet and the Peony* as well as *The Magic Pear Tree* come from his impressive body of work.

In this century fairy tales that were passed down orally from elder to child have been collected and transcribed. These usually are fairy tales that come from the peasants themselves and speak of their hardships and hopes for a better fortune. *The Greedy Brother* is such a tale.

Most recently fairy tales have been collected and adapted to reflect the Communist point of view. The final tale here, *Wild Goose Lake* is a traditional fairy tale. The theme of a young person finding a magic formula for saving his village from drought is common. But certain changes have been made. The hero is now a heroine, underlining the Communist emphasis on equality of the sexes and rejection of traditional sex roles. She is the communist person rejecting the riches that could be hers in favor of village and fellow man.

These six tales span two thousand years of Chinese history. Together they paint a portrait of a fascinating culture.

Individually they reveal a simplicity and lyric beauty that is as striking and intriguing as the country from which they have come.

HEAVEN'S REWARD

For Casey

HEAVEN'S REWARD

Yao YUN-HAO and Shia Ping-tse were best of friends. They studied under the same teacher and Shia excelled at all his tasks. Yao served him with a humble heart and in turn Shia helped him with his studies.

Despite his early achievements, Shia failed at his examinations. Soon after this he became ill and died. His family did not have the money to bury him. So faithful Yao managed to pay for the funeral and took on the burden of Shia's family, as well as his own. As his fortunes turned from bad to worse, Yao wondered how he would make his living. "If clever Shia failed, then how can I possibly succeed?" he often thought. And so Yao gave up being a scholar and went to work as a tradesman.

One day when Yao was staying at an inn, a huge man walked in and sat beside him. The man was extraordinarily tall with great muscles, though he looked pale and hungry. Yao asked if he could buy the man something to eat. When the man did not respond, Yao simply pushed over his own food to the man. He seized it and in a moment it was gone. So Yao ordered double, and this too the large man devoured. Yao ordered yet more, and this the man ate as well.

"It's three year's since I've had such a meal!" the man exclaimed.

"But you are so mighty, surely you can find work." said Yao.

"When Heaven punishes, there is nothing to be done."

"What do you mean? Where do you live?" asked Yao.

"On land I have no house, on water no boat, at dawn I am in the villages, at sunset in the cities," he replied mysteriously.

Then Yao prepared to leave but the man would not let him go. "Your life is in danger. I cannot let you go alone," said he.

The next day they were crossing a river together when a fierce wind suddenly began to blow. Waves rose and boats sank. Yao and the man were blown into the water. But the man rose up and walked on the waves, with Yao on his mighty back. As he did, the wind calmed. He placed Yao into a boat, then dived down into the water to fetch Yao's belongings. Yao thanked him over and over. "You have saved my life. And there is not a thing missing!" After this, Yao began to think that his companion was not of this earth.

When the man wished to depart, Yao pleaded with him to stay. And so the man remained. Once when speaking of the storm, Yao exclaimed, "To think that all I lost was a single gold hairpin!" With that, the man became very upset and insisted in diving into the river to find it. Yao shouted for him to return, but it was too late.

Soon after, the man reappeared with the gold hairpin in his huge hand. Yao and everyone along the riverbank marveled at the sight.

One day it grew dark and rain was about to fall. Thunder echoed through the heavens. "I wonder what clouds are and thunder is," asked Yao. "If only I could go up and see for myself. I would love to wander in the clouds." Soon after Yao grew very sleepy.

When he awoke he was no longer on a couch. Instead he was moving through the air. Clouds were all around him. The stars were so close that he could reach out and touch them. Surely this was a dream! He saw that the sky was inlaid with the stars, like little seeds on the lotus plant. The larger ones were firm in the sky, but the smaller ones shook as though they could be pulled away. Yao reached out and plucked a tiny star and hid it in his sleeve. Then the clouds parted and he could see an ocean and walled cities. He saw two dragons pulling a chariot across the skies. A vat of water sat in the chariot and men were dipping buckets into the water and sprinkling it into the clouds. One of the men was the mighty man who had saved him from the storm. "He is a friend," called the man to the other, and they handed a bucket to Yao. Yao pushed back the clouds, tried to find his village, which had long been without rain, and poured out the water with all his strength.

"I am the Thunder God's assistant" said Yao's friend. Three years ago I forgot to send rain to earth. I have been punished ever since. But now the term is ended and I must leave." Then he took a long rope from the chariot and told Yao to slide down it to earth. In moments Yao was just outside his own village. There had been a drought in his village for over three years. Now the streets were streaming with water. The ditches and drains were full at last.

Yao walked home and placed his star upon the table. By day it seemed dull and stone-like, but at night it lit his entire house.

The star shone for Yao every night. Its light never dimmed. Then one night Yao's wife noticed the light suddenly begin to fade. She opened her mouth to call Yao, and as she did the star flew right into her mouth! She tried to cough it up, but it would not come. She had swallowed a star!

That night Yao dreamed of his old friend, Shia Ping-tse. "I am now the star called *Shao-wei*," Shia said.

"I have not forgotten your kindness. Now I will give you a son."

Indeed, Yao's wife bore a son. Just before his birth, the room was filled with light. Yao and his wife called the boy Shing-erh which means "Starchild." Like Yao's old friend Shia, he grew to be a scholar. By sixteen he had passed all his official examinations.

It is said that good deeds for friends and strangers are rewarded by Heaven. In time, Heaven's rewards are made clear to all.

THE LITTLE GODDESS

*L*ONG AGO, there lived an Emperor named Po Chia. He and his Empress ruled wisely, but the gods had not seen fit to honor them with a son. This saddened them greatly as there would be no one to sit upon the Dragon Throne when Po Chia died.

And so Po Chia and his Empress went to a far away mountain to pray to the Empress of Heaven for a child. In time, three children were born to Po Chia's wife, but alas they were all daughters. The Empress grieved that no son had been born to them, but the Emperor said, "Our daughters will marry, and one of their husbands will become Emperor when I die."

His favorite daughter was named Miao Shan. He loved her dearly and so decided that it would be her husband who would become Emperor upon his death. But Miao Shan did not wish to marry.

"I do not wish to disobey you," said Miao Shan. "But the glory of being Empress is like the light of the moon reflected in a stream. Morning comes and it is gone. I wish but to sit quietly and pray to the gods. I hope to become as pure and perfect as I can. I wish to care for the sick and to help the poor. I do not want to marry and become Empress."

Her father was so angry that he took away her fine clothes and cast her out of the house to die. But the winds brought her food and the moon warmed her with its lights.

Everyone begged her to come back to the palace, but Miao Shan would not. She preferred to go to the Nunnery of the White Sparrow and live separated from the physical world.

"Let her go to the nunnery," said the Emperor. "But send word that she must be given the hardest tasks so that she will not want to become a nun."

At the nunnery Miao Shan was made to scrub floors and carry water. But Miao Shan did not complain. The Emperor of Heaven knew how good she was and so sent dragons to carry the water, a tiger to bring the heavy wood, birds to gather her vegetables. Spirits scrubbed for her and toiled for her day and night. But Miao Shan did not become lazy. She spent her time praying and helping others.

When the Emperor heard of these strange happenings he sent his troops to burn the nunnery to the ground. Miao Shan began to pray that the nunnery and its good people be spared. The smoke carried the prayers of Miao Shan up to the Emperor of Heaven. Clouds darkened and heavy rain put out the blaze.

"My daughter defies me. She must be seized and punished!" the angry Emperor cried out.

"There is a better way," said the Empress. "We will build a beautiful pavilion where Miao Shan will pass. There will be music and singing and wonderful food. Surely then she will see that our way of life is best and will give up this disobedience forever."

But good Miao Shan was not tempted. "I prefer to die and live with the gods than as Empress here on earth." Her father could not allow his daughter to disobey his wishes. And so sadly, he ordered she be seized and her head be cut off. All the court came to witness this bitter sight, but just as the axe was raised the heavens grew dark and the axe broke into pieces. And the Emperor of Heaven sent down a tiger who carried her away.

When Miao Shan awoke, she was in a dark place. There was no sun, no moon, no stars to light the sky. "You have come to the Underworld," a young man told her. "Here men are punished for the wrong they have done on earth. The Emperor of Darkness has sent me to show you his kingdom. We have heard that your prayers are so powerful they can drive away sadness and pain. May we hear such a prayer now?"

Miao Shan agreed to pray on condition that the creatures who were being punished in the Underworld be freed. Then she prayed; and as she did, the darkness began to lift. She prayed so long and hard that light filled the Underworld, and it became a paradise of beauty and light.

When Miao Shan returned to earth she met an old man who carried a gnarled stick. He placed a peach in her delicate hands. "Eat this peach," he said to her. "You will never feel hunger or thirst again. You will live forever."

Then Miao Shan ate the peach, and a great tiger, sent by the Emperor of Heaven, carried her off to an island in the Southern Sea. There Miao Shan prayed for nine years. She thought only good thoughts and in time became perfect. When this was done the Gods and Spirits of the world gathered to celebrate. She was placed on a golden throne, shaped like the precious lotus blossom. She was invited to go up to Heaven at last.

But Miao Shan was just about to enter Heaven when she heard something in the distance. It was the prayers of the millions of people who were sad or troubled on Earth. And she knew then that her place was not in Heaven but on Earth. She returned to Earth to help the troubled. And from that time on her name was changed to Gwan Yin which means "She Who Hears Prayers."

From that day to this, the people of her land have

built temples with statues of their sweet little Goddess of Mercy and Pity. And when times are troubled and sad the name Gwan Yin is often upon their lips. And it helps bring them peace for they know she is still listening to their prayers.

THE POET AND THE PEONY

$\mathcal{N}$EAR A GREAT temple on a distant mountainside, there once grew the most wondrous peonies in the world. Their blossoms were the size of large melons, their stems were twice as tall as a man, their blooms were made of solid masses of color.

One day a young poet wandered far from his town. He came upon the peonies. They were so beautiful that he decided to build a house next to them. He built his house and never went back to town.

Everyday, as he wrote, the poet gazed out at the peonies. By chance once, he caught sight of a beautiful maiden walking among the flowers. She was dressed in a trailing rose-colored gown. "Where did she come from?" the poet asked himself. Surely not from the temple on the mountainside. Only priests lived there. The

town was very far. Curious, the poet went outside to ask the maiden. But when she saw him approach, she disappeared among the flowers.

After that, the poet often saw her walking among the peonies. But no matter how quickly he ran, he could never catch up to her. He soon found himself thinking only of her. His poetry stopped like a fountain in winter. He could not sleep. Finally he decided to hide himself among the flowers and wait for her to appear. When he finally saw her coming, he stepped out of hiding and stood before her face to face. So astonished was he by her beauty, he hesitated to speak. In that moment, she turned and fled. Her rose-colored gown trailed behind her like the tailfeathers of a great bird. The poet followed and was just about to catch up when they reached the garden wall. There the mysterious maiden vanished into thin air. There was nothing but a single peony flower swaying in the wind.

The poet went back to his house. He sat down at his desk and took up his best writing brush. In his most careful writing, he wrote:

Turn not, soft flower, from the poet's hand.
He seeks to shelter you lest petals fall.

That evening as the poet sat in his house, he heard a rustling and a soft knock at his door. He rose to open it. There stood the beautiful maiden.

"Good sir," she said. "I was frightened by you, but now I know that you are a poet who loves beauty and I will no longer run from you."

"Tell me who you are, O shining maiden, and why you live among the flowers?"

"My name is Siang Yu," said she. "It is my fate to live here in the garden. Until now I have been unhappy. But now that you have come, and I find I needn't fear you, I feel happy again. May I recite a poem of my own? Please do not laugh . . ."

> *Breezes ruffle the opening bud.*
> *Oh, poet, cup your hands.*
> *I will fill them with my fragrance.*

Then the maiden hung her head in modest shame. But the poet was delighted and cried out, "Only a fool could not love you!" And so it was that the poet and the maiden found each other and came to be married.

But even after their marriage, the maiden still went out into the garden each day. While she was out, the poet wrote poems to her, which he recited every evening upon her return.

One morning, while the poet slept, the maiden prepared to leave. Tears were in her eyes as she spoke softly: "Dear friend, now the time has come for petals to fall. I fear it is the end of our life together." Then she tiptoed out.

After she had left, the poet tossed restlessly on his bed. He was dreaming that he was walking in the garden. Suddenly he came upon a gardener cutting a new path. Some flowers were in the way and so the gardener was uprooting them with a hoe. He had just pulled up a peony plant and thrown it on the ground. At that very moment, the discarded flower turned into the shape of a maiden, and the maiden's face was that of his dear Siang Yu. It was then that the poet knew his wife was really a flower spirit.

With a cry of fear, he leaped from his bed. His wife was gone. He ran into the garden. All was still. The sun was just rising. He ran further and further among the flowers until he saw a gardener. The gardener was just about to put his hoe to the roots of a rose-colored peony plant.

"Stop! Stop!" cried the poet. He ran over and pulled the hoe from the hands of the gardener. And as he did, one of the buds of the peony began to swell and open. As they watched, a little fairylike figure stepped from its rose-colored petals. The poet took the fairy and set it upon the ground. It grew and grew until it became his dear wife Siang Yu.

Then the poet sent the gardener away. He built a stone wall around the plant so that no one could carelessly destroy her. Each day Siang Yu lived in the garden, each night she returned to the house. And so they lived happily for many years. In time they died peacefully of old age. Many visitors came to see the beautiful peonies that grew in the garden. They were surprised to find a new white peony had sprung up inside the stone wall where for so many years there had only been one. Its beauty was surpassed only by the rose-colored peony which blossomed so close by.

THE GREEDY BROTHER

*T*HERE WERE once two brothers who lived in the same house. The little brother was good and hard-working though poor. The older brother and his wife were greedy and selfish though richer.

Summer had begun and it was time to sow the high-growing millet. The little brother had no grain to sow and asked his brother to lend him some. The greedy brother reluctantly agreed and ordered his wife to give some grain to his brother. But the wife first put the grain in a large pot and cooked it so it would not sprout.

The little brother knew nothing of the trick and sowed his field with this grain. Only a single sprout shot up. The little brother did not lose heart, however, the sprout grew mightily like a tree and in time a head of millet sprang up out of it.

In the fall the ear was ripe. Then the little brother took his axe and chopped down the mighty head of millet. But at the moment when it hit the ground, a tremendous bird came swooping down, took it in his beak and flew off.

The little brother would not part with his harvest so easily. He ran after the great bird right to the edge of the sea. Then he picked up stones and threw them at the bird to make him drop his load.

The bird turned toward the little brother and said, "You should not try to harm me! What is this one head of millet worth to you? East of the sea is the Isle of Gold and Silver. There are mountains of gold and valleys of silver just for the taking. I will carry you across and you may take what you will."

So the little brother climbed upon the giant bird's back. The bird commanded him to close his eyes, so he only heard the air as it whistled past his ears and the sound of crashing waves below. Then suddenly the bird settled in a rock.

The little brother opened his eyes and looked about. He was near blinded by the brilliance of the gold and silver before him. It was as if the earth itself had turned to gold and silver. He gathered up a few small pieces and hid them close to his breast.

"Have you enough?" asked the giant bird.

"Yes, I have enough," repeated the little brother.

"That is well," answered the bird. "Ask for little and you shall not be without."

When the little brother reached home, he bought himself a good piece of land with his gold and silver. He worked the land and in time became quite well off.

His older brother was jealous of his success and asked him harshly, "From where have you stolen your money?"

So the little brother told him about the giant bird and the Isle of Gold and Silver. Then the big brother went home and told everything to his wife.

"You shall repeat exactly what your little brother did. I will cook some grain, and keep back a single seed from the pot. Then you will sow it and we shall see what happens."

And sure enough, the sprout bore a single head of millet. When harvest time came, the giant bird swooped down and stole off with it. The big brother ran after the bird until he reached the edge of the shore. There he began to hurl rocks at the bird. The bird turned toward him and offered to carry him to the Isle of Gold and Silver. When he arrived, the greedy brother was astounded at the sight of its riches. He only regretted that he did not have a huge sack to fill with the loot. He bent down and began to gather as many pieces of gold and silver as he could carry.

The great bird said, "You have enough now. You will be too heavy."

"Do not be in such a hurry," protested the big brother. "I must get a few more pieces."

And time passed. The bird again urged him to make haste. "The sun will appear in a moment. Here the sun is so hot it burns up human beings."

But the big brother was not listening. His mind was on the life that would be his now that he was so rich. At that moment the red sun broke through the clouds. It was huge and flaming hot. The bird flew up, then dove into the sea, beating his wings in the water to escape the terrible heat. And the greedy brother was burned up by the sun, just as he bent over to grab one last piece of gold.

THE MAGIC PEAR TREE

*I*T WAS a blistery hot day in the ancient city. The sun beat down on the people of Shiensin. Even their broad, thick straw hats did not shade them. In the marketplace, a farmer uncovered his cart. It was filled with golden pears. They were ripe and their sweet aroma soon brought customers. By the time the sun was overhead the farmer had sold many pears. And many coins jingled deep in his pockets.

It was then that an old priest came up to the farmer. He was dressed in rags and seemed very tired and thirsty. He leaned on the cart and begged the farmer for a pear. But the farmer ignored the priest. The priest begged again. This time the farmer ordered the priest to leave the site. But the priest was persistent.

Soon the farmer was angry. His round face was flushed. He twitched in irritation. His coins jingled noisily.

"Your wagon is still full of pears," said the old priest calmly. "Your pockets are already full. Surely you can spare a single piece of fruit for a man of so many years. It is hot today, and I am tired and faint."

A crowd gathered around the farmer and the priest. They began to comment and many urged the farmer to give the priest a pear. But the farmer was stubborn. He would not give in.

"You are all generous with my property!" the farmer called out. "I do not give away pears. If you care for this priest, buy him a pear yourself!"

Then a passerby stepped forward. He gave a coin to the greedy farmer. The priest bowed low to the man. Then he took a pear from the cart and slowly ate it. As he did he spat out the seeds into his hands.

"You have all been so kind," the priest said to the crowd. "Let me show you something which will amuse you and quench our thirst."

Then he took a small shovel from his wide sleeve. He bent over and dug a hole in the dry ground. Into it, he placed a seed and covered it with earth. "I will need a pot of hot water. Will someone fetch it for me?" he called out. A young man, fond of mischief, ran off. Soon he was back with a pail of hot water.

The priest poured the hot water over the earth. A green sprout appeared. It grew and grew, until it had

27

branches with twigs and leaves. The leaves began to turn as green as the fields after a month of rain. Then pink blossoms burst forth, as beautiful as those that grow in the Emperor's famed garden. In another moment the sweet blossoms had fallen to the ground and fruit formed in their place. Hundreds and hundreds of huge pears weighed heavy in the tree's branches. The air was thick with the pungent smell of the magic tree's ripe perfect pears.

The priest reached up with his slender arm and began to pick the pears. As he did he handed them to the amazed crowd. Soon the tree was stripped completely of fruit.

When the pears had been eaten the priest took up his shovel and began to chop down the tree. In a moment its trunk lay at his feet. He bowed to the crowd, took up the tree, and walked down the street.

The farmer had watched this miraculous happening with disbelieving eyes. So amazing was it in fact that he had forgotten all about his own business. Now he let out a miserable cry.

"My pears! My pears!" he cried out. "They are all gone! Someone has robbed me of my pears." Then his eyes fell upon the handle of his cart. It had been chopped off. Upon looking farther, he found it lying nearby. It was then that he knew the pear tree had been the handle of his own cart and the luscious fruit no other than his own.

The priest was nowhere in sight. The people of

Shien-sin had gone back to work and the marketplace was now empty. The farmer would have doubted the episode were it not for the people's laughter still lingering in the hot air.

WILD GOOSE LAKE

---

*T*HERE ONCE WAS a young girl named Sea Girl who lived with her father in a town called P'o-li. A great drought had dried the local canals that watered the fields of P'o-li. The harvest had not survived and far and near people were starving.

One day Sea Girl walked to the top of Horse Ear Mountain. She had been walking a long time when she suddenly saw a huge shining lake. The lake's water was as clear and smooth as glass. Not a single fallen leaf disturbed its surface. Each time a leaf drifted onto the lake, a wild goose swept down and carried it away. Sea Girl had come upon the Wild Goose Lake. The lake was so beautiful and peaceful that it seemed to be the home of great spirits. Sea Girl watched for some time as the wild geese collected leaves. When the sun was beginning to pass behind the mountains, she finally went home. But in her mind were images of the Wild Goose Lake. She knew there had to be a way to get its life-giving water to the drought-stricken people below.

The next day Sea Girl went back to the Wild Goose Lake. Upon her shoulder she carried an axe. Sea Girl was determined to make an outlet so that the lake's water could flow down to her village's empty canals. For half a day she walked around the lake. It was surrounded by mountains and forests. At last she came upon a stone gate. Five red stones in a circle decorated its lock. Sea Girl hacked at the gate and its lock for many hours, but it would not budge. Finally, she gave up and sat down under the shade of a tree and looked out onto the lake's gleaming waters. There had to be some way to open the stone gate and let loose the waters of the Wild Goose Lake.

Just then one of the wild geese landed beside her.

"Sea Girl, Sea Girl," said the bird. "You need the sixth red stone to open the lock of the Wild Goose Lake," and it flew away.

But where was the sixth red stone? The bird had flown away before she could ask. Sea Girl stood up and began to walk along the northern shore of the lake, where she came to a cypress forest. There she saw three colorful parrots.

"Parrots, parrots," said the young girl. "Where

can I find the sixth red stone to open the lock of the Wild Goose Lake?"

"Sea Girl, Sea Girl," answered the three parrots, "You must find the third daughter of the Dragon King." So Sea Girl kept walking along the shore wondering where she could find the Dragon King's third daughter. When she came to the western side of the lake she saw a magnificent peacock.

"Peacock, peacock," said she, "Where can I find the Dragon King's third daughter?" And the peacock said:

"Sea Girl, Sea Girl, sometimes she sings on the southern shore."

The peacock spread his brilliant wings and flew to the south and Sea Girl followed. At last the bird landed in a cinnamon tree. Sea Girl looked all around but she did not see the Dragon King's third daughter.

The peacock said, "Sea Girl, Sea Girl, the third daughter lives beneath the waters of the Wild Goose Lake, but she sometimes rises up to sing. Perhaps if you sing the songs the people sing, she will come forth." The peacock spread his wings once more and was gone.

So Sea Girl walked along the sandy shore until she came to the eastern edge of the lake. There she sat down and began to sing. On the first day she sang about the snowflakes upon the southern mountains, but the Dragon King's third daughter did not appear. On the second day she sang about the green grass that

grew along the lake, but still the third daughter did not come. On the third day Sea Girl sang about the blossoming flowers that grew along the surrounding hills. She sang so long that the blazing sun finally disappeared behind the western mountain.

Suddenly a girl rose up from the center of the Wild Goose Lake. Her hair was long and entwined with shells, her robes were spun of seaweed and her skin was the color of pearls. It was the Dragon King's third daughter. The Dragon King had strictly forbidden his daughters to mingle with the living world. But the third daughter loved to sing and she heard Sea Girl's songs. Each day she had listened. Finally on the third day she could stand it no longer and rose up out of the water when no one was near.

"Where do you live?" she asked Sea Girl. "Why do you come here to sing each day?"

"My name is Sea Girl. I live in P'o-li, the village at the foot of Horse Ear Mountain. I am searching for the sixth red stone to release the water of the Wild Goose Lake to help my drought-stricken people."

The good-hearted third daughter replied, "The sixth stone is in my father's treasury. A big eagle guards it. The eagle would kill anyone, except my father, who dared to enter it. Only when the king leaves the palace could one possibly get into the treasury. Wait for me each evening when the sun hides behind the mountains. I will come to you when he is gone."

So every evening Sea Girl waited beside the Wild

35

Goose Lake. Then one day Third Daughter rose up from the lake. Together they descended into the clear water. When they arrived at the Dragon King's palace, Sea Girl realized that she could breathe quite easily and, though she was under water, she was not at all wet. She gazed about her in awe. Never had she seen such splendor. The palace walls were made of the greenest jade and its floors were of the whitest marble. The door to the treasury was bronze and silver. Beside it sat an old eagle sleeping.

Sea Girl and Third Daughter stood before the great door and began to sing. At first the eagle remained asleep and did not seem to hear the music. But after some time he began to rouse. He opened his wings and looked about to see who was singing. At that moment Sea Girl slipped into the treasury to look for the sixth red stone.

The treasury was ablaze with the blinding light of gold and silver. It was filled with glimmering pieces of jewelry, brilliant rare pearls, glittering gold. But Sea Girl thought little of these riches. She thought instead of the scorching sun and the cool water of the Wild Goose Lake. But look as she may, she could not find the red stone. In her despair, she knocked against a highly polished carved wood box. The box fell over and out tumbled a single red stone. Hastily, Sea Girl picked up the stone and ran out of the treasury before the eagle could see her.

Together Third Daughter and Sea Girl left the

watery palace of the Dragon King. They journeyed up, higher and higher, until at last they came to the still surface of the Wild Goose Lake. When they reached the shore they headed straight for the stone gate that held back the lake's water. Sea Girl placed the stone into the huge lock. The gate opened slowly and the water began to stream forth. Within minutes the canals below were overflowing with the clear water of the Wild Goose Lake. But as if by magic the lake remained just as full as before.

When the Dragon King returned, he discovered that the sixth stone was gone and that his third daughter had been the living world. In anger, he banished Third Daughter from the palace. But rather than pleading with her father to remain, Third Daughter gladly rose up from the waters of Wild Goose Lake and went to live with her friend Sea Girl and her father, Chiao.

And it is said that if you go to the top of Horse Ear Mountain beside the Wild Goose Lake, where geese pluck leaves from its surface to keep it clear as crystal, there you can hear the voices of Sea Girl and the Dragon King's third daughter raised in glorious song.